Patrick Cudmore

President Grant and political rings

A satire

Patrick Cudmore

President Grant and political rings
A satire

ISBN/EAN: 9783337134327

Printed in Europe, USA, Canada, Australia, Japan

Cover: Foto ©Andreas Hilbeck / pixelio.de

More available books at **www.hansebooks.com**

PRESIDENT GRANT

AND

POLITICAL RINGS

A SATIRE.

BY P. CUDMORE. ESQ.,

COUNSELOR AT LAW.

Author of the " Civil Government of the States, and the
Constitutional History of the United States,"
the " Irish Republic," etc., etc.

NEW YORK:

For Sale by P. J. KENEDY, No. 5 Barclay Street.

1880.

PRESIDENT GRANT:

A SATIRE.

Appomattox surrender made **Grant** a hero—
He was dubbed a Scipio and a Cæsar—
He was not noble, great, nor even grand,
His selfish avarice was his god!
With Johnson he proved a double dealer
And joined a ring of Republican schemers.
In 1868 for President he was then run—
As a candidate both deaf and dumb.
Of all the spirits that Christ scourged
The dumb devil was hardest to purge.
Grant displayed cunning and deceit,
In his letter of "Let us have peace."
When in power, peace was then treason,
His argument was th' bullet and bayonet.
Before election it was his proud boast,
That he had no " policy of his own,"
But when in office he changed his tone.
By him th' Constitution was o'erthrown.
His word was law—and avarice his rule ;

As the mother hen gathers her chickens under her wing—
The President's pardon was a good thing—
And as the hen to her chicks doth cluck,
Grant with his pardon th' birds did hush up.
When McKey was caged th' *Democrat* did rant,
And Grant was afraid they'd cage his Bab.,
And that th' jail birds would blab, blab, blab.
Bristow and the courts did Bab. alarm—
He'd a military commission in Chicago.
Hancock and others—good men and true men,
Sent Bab. and his imps back to St. Louis ;
Judge Treat was filling up the prison,
And as a dead weight Grant sent 'em Dillon.
When Grant saw that Bab. would be caged,
He trembled for Orville—his heart did ache.
Off to St. Louis his detective did hie,
To steal from the U. S. Attorney evidence on file—
Whiskey conspirators weren't then alarmed,
For the President withdrew th' "State's-evidence pardon."
Because Gen. Custer testified 'gainst the ringers,
He was sent on th' plains to be scalped by Indians.
The Attorney-Gen'ral, the vile old sinner,
Instead of prosecuting Bab. became his defender,
The President's power—oh, jury and Dillon,
Bab. th' whiskey conspirator was finally acquitted—
The power of the President was so great,
Bab.'s indictment was hushed up for *"blowing up a safe."*
And before the President's term did end,
He opened th' jail-door and let the birds out to sing.
In 1875, Grant and his vile abettors,

Electioneered for a Presidential third term ;
If he'd got a third he'd want a fourth one,
He'd be a dictator like Cæsar or Napoleon.
His imperial airs were so unusual,
That he would play Cæsar in the future—
His military power was so despotic,
That th' people feared th' man on horseback.
A third nomination doubtless he'd win,
But for Belknap, Babcock, and the whiskey ring.
His military renown was daily waning,
Before Congressional Committee investigation.
The people's confidence in Grant had diminished,
When they saw the President shielding whiskey ringers.
In 1876, Jim Blaine made a great splurge,
In Congress he flaunted his bloody shirt,
He would be nominated for President, certain,
But for the lobbyists and " Mulligan letters."
Morton, Butler, and other wily knaves,
" *Put up the job* " to slaughter Jim Blaine.
Between Republican aspirants rivalry was great—
As a compromise candidate they ran Hayes.
Grant feared that by Tilden he'd be investigated,
He tried to carry the election by soldiers and bayonets.
Instead of keeping the army at the Black Hills,
He sent them South to bulldoze " the colored men."
Grant proved a traitor in the " *Alabama Claims,*"
A dupe in San Domingo and Samana Bay.
In 1869 Grant joined in the bond-holders plan,
By signing the bill for the bond-holding clan.
A bill for paying the five-twenties in gold.

Thus, out of the Treasury millions were *stole*.
In 1873 Grant showed his mean folly,
By demonetizing our silver dollar.
When Grant was President, the people were alarmed,
When the Southern States were governed by satraps,
Carpet-bag governors he upheld by bayonets,
In South Carolina, Scott, Moses and Chamberlain.
In Louisiana his "military rule" was despotic,
The ballot-box was overthrown by Kellogg and Packard.
Republican papers cried "Oh, Hamburg!"
In South Carolina rifle clubs were disbanded,
His military orders were despotic, unusual—
A violation of State rights and the Constitution.
On the State Governors Grant did frown,
He'd supplant self-government by military power.
In his Southern policy he stood alone.
He knew no laws but military force—
In his policy to protect "the colored man,"
He put the South under military ban.
Grant, the tyrant, triumphed o'er the law,
Like Pisastratous, he had a body-guard.
To use intimidation and bribery at the ballot-box,
Federal officers were taxed by Chandler and Cameron.
From the North there was a carpet-baggers' flood
Of men who left their country for their country's good,
For during this fierce political strife,
Carpet-baggers robbed the people—"black and white."
To purge the carpet-bag rule from the Southern States,
Caused the colored stampede to Tilden from Hayes.
After election the Republicans found it out,

That Grant's misrule united the " *Solid South.*"
Republicans grief and spite were very great,
When they found Tilden elected over Hayes.
Grant, Chamberlain and Cameron, and other rogues,
Kept Tilden out of office by " Returning Boards."
Grant's tactics was a military display,   .
To bull-doze the Democrats and inaugurate Hayes
His military display alarmed the Nation ;
In South Carolina he ousted the legislature,
In Louisiana he followed up his military tactics,
With troops he supported Kellogg and Packard.
Chandler and Cameron laid the wires and ropes,
To get fraudulent certificates from Returning Boards.
In Florida, South Carolina, carpet-bag States,
Fraudulent electors were returned for Hayes.
When the Republicans found themselves beaten,
They cried out " bull-dozing " and "intimidation!"
The canvassing-boards, their deputies and clerks,
Had contested returns compiled in the dark.
The Returning Board of the State of Louisiana,
Offered to sell out for a million dollars.
In South Carolina, Florida and Louisiana,
The Returning Boards ousted towns and parishes.
In the three last mentioned carpet-bag States,
Democratic parishes were thrown out to give certificates to
         Hayes.
Grant was the first President to employ military law,
Hayes the first President chosen by fraud.
In the memorable year of the Nation's Centennial,
There were two Presidential aspirants, Hayes and Tilden.

The Democrats said they elected Tilden and Hendricks,
The Republicans said that Grant would make Hayes winner.
The fear of another war had alarmed the Nation,
The people feared the presidential question would end with bayonets,
They said that fifteen would settle our political trouble.
The Democrats squirmed under eight to seven.
Tilden and Hewitt thought they were a match for Hayes,
But they found their seven swallowed up by eight.
The people were astounded to behold the new plan,
When the president of forty-five millions was chosen by one man.
The Democrats cried out it was deceit at the best,
But if victors, in future, they must fly to the West—
Beware of all political hacks, tricksters and schemers,
Trust not in empty promises in the year eighty—
We will have our chief magistrate elected by ballot,
Not by Returning Boards—Wells, Morton and Bradley,
The President in future must be elected by ballot.
We will abolish the nuisance, the Electoral College,
The people will then assume their sovereignty ;
The majority in future shall rule the minority.
Grant, when first elected, had military fame,
He left the White House in a cloud of shame.
He went to Galena, where he was a tanner,
And then to England to see Mrs. Sartoris.
Mrs. Grant was all fidget and racket,
Preparing to sail by the very next packet.
Grant, in London, put on princely airs,

He bowed his head to the rich and great,
He got receptions from Ministers of State—
A reward for his treason with Alabama Claims—
In his speeches to John B—— he had the folly
To pledge Columbia as a British ally.
The Galena tanner in pompous state,
Hob-nobbed to Victoria and the Prince of Wales.
He is the first President with the brand,
Of putting on royal airs in foreign lands !
Grant appeared in uniform—military traps,
He acted the Lickspittle—a military fop.
He danced attendance on lords and dukes.
He had an invitation each day in June—
He would act Cæsar or a Mogul,
And for a commission he'd turn Turk.
Oh, what a time had the Galena tanner,
Taking a drive in Victoria's fine carriage!
He despised his countrymen as serfs,
While wining and dining with the stupid guelphs.
John B—— cared little for Grant's folly,
Only he wanted Uncle Sam for an ally.

POLITICAL RINGS:

A SATIRE.

By P. CUDMORE, Esq.,

COUNSELOR-AT-LAW.

Author of the "Civil Government of the States and the Constitutional
History of the United States," the "Irish Republic," etc., etc.

POETS of yore to Parnassus did wing—
And invoked the muses to aid 'em to sing—
Their themes often were grand and sublime.
Some like Dante hurled shafts of satire—
Others writ of heroic deeds—chieftains and kings.
My theme is corruption and political rings—
Politicians have form'd rings in ev'ry place—
And a Canal ring in th' Empire State.
Rings in ev'ry county, town, city, and ward,—
There was a corrupt ring in Tammany Hall.
Connolly, Sweeney, Tweed, and their pals,
Were indicted for corruption and fraud.
They thought that their deeds ne'er would be known,
For they controll'd th' Legislature and th' Courts.
And although Tweed possessed millions,
O'Conor and th' "Seventy" sent 'im to prison—

To rob Uncle Sam is a profitable thing,
And in Washington is a Treasury ring.
There are rings of distillers and gaugers,
Bab.'s conspiracy was in Grant's chamber—
The rings had their aiders and abettors,
A Washington ring was headed by Shepherd—
By Court-House rings the people are defrauded.
There was a corrupt ring in Chicago—
There are treasury defaulters in th' States all o'er,
And S——, and M——, in Minnesota.
Tweed for his frauds to prison did go—
A defalcation, in Minnesota, is called a "*lone.*"
There are rings to rob the poor red man—
There were rings of schemers to evade the draft.
Rings for stealing in the public lands,
And a ring for stealing by "*railroad bonds.*"
Rings of schemers, rogues, and defrauders,
And many rings for robbing the farmers.
Rings of lobbyists, strikers—political thieves.
And railroad rings—and the "*Credit Mobilier.*"
Rings for stealing in the State school funds,
And rings for monopoly in school books—
And rings for stealing in the swamp lands,
And rings for stealing in school fund bonds,
Rings for stealing from the poor Indians,
And rings of defaulters—agents of pensions;
In the pension office was a big steal,
Jim B——r, in Chicago, bulldozed Miss Sweet—
There were rings of trappers and Indian traders,
And rings to buy up Territorial Legislatures,

Rings for stealing in the State pine lands,
And a ring for th' payment of railroad bonds.
Rings of gaugers and inspectors of stills—
Millions are stolen by "Crooked Whiskey" rings.
Revenue thieves make a very big thing—
And in New York is a Custom-house ring.
In ev'ry legislature are lobby ringers,
And in Minnesota are railroad skinners—
Rings of bondholders and railroad agents,
Skinners by name and skinners by nature.
Mc—— made a fortune in pine land stumps,
And built a huge mansion with "State funds."
Th' Government is robbed by contractors and builders,
They are aided by army and naval ringers—
Rings influence men in high and low station,
And railroad rings the State Legislatures—
Rings for reconstructing th' Southern States,
And Grant's conspiracy to inaugurate Hayes—
Many rings of miners and land grabbers,
And rings of speculators—"railroad wreckers,"
And rings for cheating in wheat and oats
And for defrauding th' Gov't by cancelling its notes.
And although th' rings did plunder and steal,
Th' President and Governors did 'em shield.
Many were indicted for "huge steals"—
Th' prosecution increased th' debts of th' States.
None ev'r doubted of their plunder and fraud,
Money and party triumphed o'er th' laws.
And where th' dominant party didn't want investigation
Th' matter was hushed up by accepting a resignation—

To cover up frauds and stealings Juries are packed
And State and County Attorneys wink at th' job—
And when to prison was sent a rogue or defaulter,
The Jail door was opened by th' President's pardon.
There are rings and defaulters in ev'ry station
And corruption and plunder all o'er th' nation.
Oh, for a Jefferson, a Jackson, or a Clay !
We have mere politicians—has virtue failed ?

A COURT-HOUSE RING.

A SATIRE.

In this poem, I am not over civil
M—— D——, stands for "Mike the Devil."
With vile politicians he was in Co—
So you may call him Buck or Do.
My theme is n't of faries, heroes, or princes,
But of one o' th' vilest of vile politicians.
D—— was not known to the rulers of nations;
In Kilkenny (——) he took up his station.
When he enter'd politics, he was no expert,
Till he became an apprentice to Beelzebub.
Bubby tutored him in lies and deceit,
Till he eclips'd the serpent that tempted Eve.
This C—— hack had a battalion of spies,
He defeat'd Doyle and D——ty with deceit and lies.
This trickster had no love for pigeon or dove,
In his greed he gulp'd down Kilkenny's sweet bird;
With lies, corruption, he stirred up contention;
He was an adept at packing a convention.
Satan, with a smile, said to old Do,
"For Greenbacks you sell the county's Gold;"
For well you know how to grab up pelf,
You may keep the profit to yourself.

Said Do to Satan, "I'll do it smart."
So with th' county's gold he got his first start.
His satyric phiz had a smile satanic,
When he defeated poor John L. Meagher.
While handling S——'s money he felt very big—
With promises and lies he defeated Bill Smith.
Bill was undaunted (——), he was a trump,
And rather than yield he ran on th' stump.
Do for to match 'im and cause him to stumble,
With the aid of Dick Walsh he ran Frank Quinlan.
Frank was jovial, jolly, and easy ;
With dangling curls he charmed some ladies ;
But the dangling curls have fled, alas !
Who now cares for Doran's poor old Ass?
Franky was lazy (——), he drank "much sack,"
It will cost a million for his clerk.
Let Frank cry, "Commune"—and "tramp, tramp,"
He's a dearer pill than th' bogus bonds.
I remember how Frank's heart did flutter
When he was pursu'd by Tim for th' buggy.
M—— D—— ground his teeth and he swore like Satan,
When he was defeated by Luther Z. Rogers.
D—— had at command men of all brands,
He'd a brace of supporters in Cadwell and Bangs.
With his victories he felt quite inflated,
He was ready to burst like th' toad in th' fable.
Though a mere lout and ignorant boor,
He became ambitious of honor and fame ;
And, in his pride, he aspired to an office of State.
By packing conventions he got a delegation,
And for State Auditor he got a nomination.
Fearing some light—he signed his resignation.
He got a plotting—and by deception and scheming,
He thought to get to Congress or some high station.
Though not gifted as a debater or orator,

He'd make a mark as a striker (———) Salary Grabber.
To make th' road clear for his political plans,
He laid his traps to defeat McDonald and Cox.
In all o' his scheming, early and late,
He was a mere tool of Horace B. Strait.
As long as th' fox runs he is captured at last—
Cudmore, th' historian, let th' cat out of th' bag.
Do an apprentice of old Beelzebub,
Finds his Congressonal honors (———) a bubble of suds.
In 1875 Do elected Frank Kolars ;
In 1876 his *Jim* was defeated by Borer.
Through Kilkenny this hopeful was in a sputter,
Drumming up votes for mere bread and butter.
M—— D—— cared little for friend, cousin, brother ;
With "no Irish need apply" he defeated Tom Byrne.
This miserable boor was bloated with pride—
Like a hawk on a bird he pounced on M. Wilds.
In th' Legislature Do defeated Mark for Superintendent,
For bringing to light Do's figures while Treasurer.
Mark felt indignant at th' loss of his station,
And as County Commissioner su'd Do for ———.
Bangs was dejected—th' county employed Cox—
On th' eve of election Le Sueur was "nolle pros."
When M—— D—— goes through th' county puppies do
    bark,
They feel so indignant for th' dogs that he taxed.
To get the County Seat to th' Centre puzzled his wit,
Till he got th' aid of Rogers, Mort, and E. Smith.
Back again to Le Sueur th' officials he'd quarter,
And sell for a poor-house his building, farm.
The County officials he put under tribute—
He laid it thick on Quinlan, Kolars, Kinsey—
His man Friday—fugleman in every season,
Was his ready tool—bald-headed Mike Gr——y.
Mike was not active at capturing thieves,

He knew enough figures to multiply fees.
Old Mike, the Sheriff (———) a man of straw,
In the Court-house stands (———) a pipe in his jaw.
What a phiz—sniff—snivel—snuffle—sneeze!
He lost th' hair of his head adding fees.
Where to place Me I am at my wits end,
And for th' present he may straddle th' fence.
Th' fear of bodly harm troubled D——'s mind,
He sent to St. Peter honest Bill Dynes.
In 1867, D—— for Treasurer did run—
To head him off, John ran on the stump.
In 1875, Do devis'd th' Satanic plan,
Th' defeat o' Borer with political hacks.
C—— was defeated by political tricksters.
The cry of the ring was, "stick to the ticket;"
Then, to defeat C——, the Court-house pack
All united from Do to ———,
O'er political blood-hounds Do's whip did crack,
G——y, Q——, M——y, and "Jim" joined th' pack.
With literary talent Do was not bless'd,
Yet, in Le Sueur, he bulldozed th' press.
M—— D——, for the bonds, didn't know how to vote.
He consulted C——n, not a judge of a court.
Those he didn't enlist with promises and ———
He united his dupes like Satan with lies.
During the war he was a man-catcher—trap—
He joined a ring for evading the draft.
M—— D——, Capt. C——, and Dr. Mayo,
To evade the draft, met in Faribault.
That mean vile crew, with satanic skill,
Out of poor men did their pockets fill.
They had their runners—man-catchers—traps—
Who made believe they'd exempt from th' draft.
Their delud'd dupes in numbers flocked,
And gave th' draft ring thousands in greenbacks.

The mean, vile, low ring made the mare go,
And for greenbacks fleeced friend and foe.
As a billy goat scampers down hill,
D—— ran off from Marshal Averill.
Like the vile arch fiend fallen from bliss,
Do's sole delight was in doing amiss.
To set up his pins securely and strong,
He made nominations in Le —— bank.
While playing billiards (———-) drinking in grog shops,
He selected his tools for packing caucuses—
He rode through the county to mature his plans ;
He used beer and whisky and a low dance.
When he found men more practical than funny,
With the beer and th' dance he gave them m——y.
He employed craft, malice, envy (———) double dealing ;
Ambiguity—tricks—deceit—promises—scheming.
To rule or ruin he'd use money and spies,
And, like Satan, mix truth "to vent more lies."
He dissembled (——), the rich he worshiped and praised ;
He looked on foes with anger and low disdain.
His duped followers oft he did beguile,
With fair promises and satanic lies.
He seldom or never prayed to the most High ;
He bent his knee to Satan and Belial ;
He car'd not for heroes—not Agamemnon ;
A mean hunk he—hunker-like worship'd Mammon.
For wealth and power he had a thirst,
He took Satan's counsel—" Get money first."
For to get wealth (-- ——) his motto was, " succeed."
In deceit, lies, and cunning he eclipsed th' fiend.
This greedy cormorant cared not for God's law,
If with filthy lucre he could fill his maw.
To get votes or to reap more gain,
He'd worship Satan's God—even Baal.
He was outlandish, base, mean, and vile ;

Even the truth he mixed with lies.
Th' trickster thinks that by means of pelf,
That to Congress he will go himself.
Th' trickster to Congress ne'er will go,
Be his reward of merit th' hangman's rope!
Indeed, the slave has his tools and spies,
And he pulls his puppets with his wires.
Now, to this trickster a word I say—
That every mean dog has his day!

DORAN'S ASS--1878.

Franky, indeed, was quite a mean one—
He turned Turk—he turned Bohemian ;
Not, indeed, for what he ev'r had "wrote,"
But for packing caucuses—trading votes.
Franky to his friends never was true ;
To gain a voter he would lose two.
He was with all parties on all questions ;
He was false to his friends ; he us'd deception ;
To get elected was his aim and end.
For a few votes he would sell his friends.
At conventions how he raves and rants,
That noisy, toady and silly Frank!
How the people listen when they pass,
Just to hear the bray of Doran's ass!!
That stupid ass, in his pranks one day,
From his cruel master ran away ;
But the noisy, stupid, servile, hack,
Just when Doran whistled, hurried back.
He stooped down at his master's crack,
To get his burden put on his back.
While he stood mute at his master's rack,
He was told the convention he should pack ;

That he should work, then canter and bray,
While his cruel master was at th' fair.
Just wait awhile till election day,
This stupid ass will want more fresh hay.
When this stupid donkey will want oats,
Or in other words, the people's votes,
Tell this donkey, when for votes he asks,
You can go to thistles—"go to grass!"
A bald-headed sheriff, with a frown,
Said the "ticket with Irish don't load down!"
This d——, this s——, of the Irish nation,
By Irishmen's votes got his high station.
This mean hack for Doran loudly bawls—
In seventy-nine he'll have a fall.
The donkey's blood-hounds, Doran's vile pack,
The people will clear from th' election track.
'Stick to the ticket," is th' cry of th' hacks;
Let the people shout, "Vote for greenbacks!"
When he wants votes, Doran's hack doth whine,
Don't you forget, " No Irish need apply!"
He'd keep Irishmen from office, the mean elf;
Let th' rule be applied, then, to himself.

M—— D——'s study early and late,
Was to get office, real estate—
To get pelf, power—office—civil,
He sold himself unto the devil!
The contract was drawn with devil's skill,
Was writ in blood with a raven's quill.
To get knowledge from Beelzebub,
He drank raven's blood from a raven's skull—
Bird of darkness—ill-omen—evil—
D——'s companion is the devil.
The Black Crook, or fiend of sable night,
Will take (D——) to his kingdom in his flight.

The vile arch-fiend employed his skill,
And tutored D—— to manage the mill.
When by "hocus-pocus, presto, pass,"
The mill stockholders then "went to grass."
The fiend worked hard, early and late,
And gave M—— office, wealth, real estate.
Th' evil one's power he did employ,
That his enemies he could defy.
They say the devil must have his due—
Others joined M—— D——'s vile crew ;
For to gain influence and capture votes,
D——, with Lapland witches, rode a goat.
The mean dregs of every nation
Worked for D—— for wealth or station ;
This vile, low herd—this mean, servile pack—
Always ready when M——'s whip did crack.
Those that the fiend raised always fell ;
D—— and his crew may go to h—ll.
Before you vote think awhile and stop ;
In Le Sueur is a "put-up job."
If you vote for Doran's servile hacks,
You will have the bonds upon your backs ;
You will have to work hard night and day,
The bogus railroad bonds for to pay!
Fearing that C—— would run on th' stump,
D—— met his asses at the town pump ;
At th' town pump they joined in marriage.
Seventy-nine there'll be a miscarriage!
The people 'll have a very long rest ;
There will be a divorce of the pests.
D—— ground his teeth with a great frown ;
He said, "Iv'e asses in every town."
His donkeys were running night and day,
And palsy-headed *Jack* made a loud bray ;
O'er th' county it was gallop and trot ;

What a mean donkey was lying Jack!
In ev'ry town he had hacks and spies ;
Blatherskite *Jack* told a bundle of lies.
Ill it fared with poor old Do,
That his insane job was no go.
To congress he cannot now sail,
On his last hobby, th' county jail.
Down, down, down-hill he now must slide—
Th' state prison hobby he can't ride.
For his mean, low Kasota trick,
In the next race he will break his neck.

Old Frank was mean, low, and wicked,
For he burned John Harty's greenback ticket.
Now he is on the election track,
With a load of sin upon his back.
After election Franky will weep,
On his very long trip up Salt Creek!
On the stump th' ring thought C—— too bluff,
And one of the gang was Deacon Killduff.
Th' political hacks will meet their doom ;
They will be swept from office with a broom.
The ring will yet come to grief and shame
For imputing greenbackers insane.
A judgment will follow their mean tricks ;
They or their friends will be lunatics.
For their low cunning, deceit, falsehood,
The court-house rats will shed tears of blood.
Stewart met with sorrow, grief, and woe,
When M—— D—— he joined in Co.
What a sad, dismal tale he can tell ;
He paid for his lesson very well!
The plan is now laid—the trap is set—
Another victim is in the net.
M—— D—— will live as he had begun –
The wretch 'll die " unhonored and unsung ! "

1 8 7 9.

At Cleveland, said the mean boor and scamp,
In th' Senate, "I'll pass a law 'gin tramps."
The mean boor through the county did tramp,
To get good Irishmen to sign his bond.
Some banks will break like the ocean surge ;
The boor's offspring will yet tramp and drudge.
A judgment will follow the boor soon ;
His wealth 'ill shingle many a saloon.
Now the booby the poor doth deride,
Behold the swagger of the upstart's pride.
In the Senate the boor cried, "peculation!"
Did he forget his gold speculation?
The brazen upstart, was he not pert,
In the Senate to talk of experts?
Of all the humbugs since creation
Is a Le Sueur investigation.
"Loose book-keeping" (——), ink, and botches,
Le Sueur (——) books, scratches, scratches.
In the court-house are some Doran hacks ;
They are known in th' county as "the Franks."
There is Frank the sly, and Frank the fop ;
I'll not forget Frank, the mean yellow dog.
M—— D——'s hacks are human chattel,
Which he drives like "dumb, driven cattle."
The boor on big interest was intent ;
In th' Senate he voted for a big per cent.
(——) fixing interest at ten per cent.—so—
In the Senate he voted no, no, no !
M—— D—— made a sad mistake
When he aspired to dictator of th' State.
Like the tortoise that want'd to fly,
Flat on the ground he now must lie.

The eagle may soar toward heaven ;
But on th' ground reptiles find their level.
In Chicago it was D——'s intention
To make a splurge in the convention ;
At th' *Times'* reporter he'd spit and spat ;
He bristled up like a big tom cat.
Oh, what a horrid look—what a sight!
D——'s big grin—but he could not bite ! !

M—— D——'S EPITAPH.

M——- D—— lies beneath this clod of earth,
  A boor to honor and to truth unknown ;
Under the dragon's tail was his mishap birth,
  And Be-el-ze-bub claimed him for his own.

THE BONDHOLDER'S LAMENTATION.

A SATIRE.

———•◦•———

THE people were victors on election day—
The bondholders set up a lament or a wail ;
They called an election on the 12th day of June (1877),
But they did not find that the farmers were fools.
The bondholders and their understrappers
Did not find that the farmers were nappers.
The bondholders' press set up a wild bray—
"You vot'd down th' bonds"—of light you've not a ray.
To those who vot'd for th' bonds, it said "all right,
You're moral men in the splendor of light"—
To the farmers it said, " you mean stupid serfs,
You're mean and ignorant for not taxing yourselves."
A bondholder's paper—a friend of the ringers,
Said, " vote for the bonds or you are vile sinners."
If you don't dance to the bondholder's tune,
You're worse than infidels and the Commune.
Those who advocate th' payment of bogus bonds
Are helping to confiscate the farmer's lands.
'Tis 'gainst th' law of God and th' law of nature,
To take th' farmer's lands by confiscation.
It is a legal maxim, well understood,
"That treason doesn't work corruption of the blood."

Even for acts of treason and rebellious strife,
You can only confiscate the farms for life.
You who cry repudiation and divine law,
Know that the farmers haven't committed treason at all.
Those who call railroad bonds " an honest debt,"
Delude others or they delude themselves.
Jefferson, Madison, and Monroe took a stand
Against giving railroads a bonus or land.
Th' Constitutional fathers, in their time,
Held such donations illegal and unwise.
Th' bondholder's press is keeping up a wild bray,
That hereafter the bogus bonds we must pay.
Farmers, heed not this false siren's note,
You'll not pay the bonds till for 'em you vote.
If you heed th' bondholders and their brib'd hacks,
You'll yet groan under a mountain of tax.
If you don't vote for the bondholder's tax,
They'll say you're benighted and live in the dark.
Chamberlain will follow C—— D——'s plan,
Th' legislature to make a haul or a grab.
You now ask me how this can be done,
By a bill to grab the State school fund.
If you send th' bondholders to make the laws,
They will grab the school bonds by trick or fraud.
Heed you this wise adage oft time spoken,
You lock th' stable door when th' horse is stolen.
The bondholders will devise a scheme—·
Political hacks for a court of claims ;
Th' bondholders know what that court will say,
For Chamberlain has Greenbacks to pay.
Farmers, beware of railroad bond ringers ;
You know how you'll vote on next November.

TAXES.

A SATIRE.

In this age of civilization
The people are slaves to taxation ;
Th' politicians have made man a slave,
To toil and moil from th' cradle to th' grave.
The people are tax'd for clothes and food,
And for house, furniture, coal, and wood ;
They are tax'd for matches (————), e'en a pill,
What a heavy tax is the doctor's bill!
That tax the people pay with a will,
Is the tax on the worm of the still.
They are tax'd (————) from a nail to a rope,
And for tobacco that they puff in smoke.
They're tax'd for tools (————) implements of trade ;
They are tax'd for soap and the barber's blade.
The farmer is tax'd for th' team he drives,
He's tax'd for the road o'er which he rides,
He's tax'd for his mower, rake, and thresher,
And for his pump, cradle, and his washer,
He is tax'd for his mill and reaper,
And from a grind-stone to a seeder.

He's tax'd for the produce of his lands,
And he is taxed for railroad bonds.
He is taxed by the thieving rings,
Despots worse than many tyrant kings.
He is taxed for his clock and gun,
And for all he owns beneath the sun.
He is taxed to make or mend the law ;
He feeds soldiers both in peace and war.
He is tax'd to feed those that rule,
And for to feed the wicked and the poor.
He is tax'd to feed the mute and blind,
And the rogue and those who've no mind.
To pay taxes he is sorely driven—
He supports the school, church, and prison.
He is taxed for the books that he reads,
For all creation, but the air he breathes.
The people boast of their colleges and schools,
Yet, they are ruled by knaves and tools.
We've a free press and civilization—
We're (——) tax-ridden people since creation.
Th' people 'll pay big taxes and booty,
While they vote for a knave or booby.
Th' tax ridden people will take a stand,
They'll tax railroads and the railroad land.
It will free millions from starvation
To tax moneyed corporations.
Tax monopolists and moneyed kings,
Bondholders, usurers, and the gold rings.
It would take th' burden off th' people's backs,
To lay on a heavy income tax.
Indeed, the farmers will the day rue,
That they kept in office th' knave and boor.
What better than a thief and robber
Is th' court-house rat and salary grabber ?
The farmers vote for their old party hacks,

Who put a load of tax upon their backs.
The farmer is taxed for th' coffin in which he sleeps ;
He is taxed for shroud and winding sheets.
In the grave the farmer is taxed still,
For there is a heavy tax on his *will*.
In the grave he isn't free from taxation,
For his *will* is taxed for probation.
He's tax'd in this world and (———) future state ;
He's tax'd on the road to heaven's gate.
When will he be free from the tax bill ?
Just when good Saint Peter lets him in.

"The Day we Celebrate."

---- •••• ----

Irishmen celebrate this day in ev'ry land,
From th' bright polar star to th, southern cross ;
From Labrador to India's coral strand,
And from th' gigantic Andes to th' classic Alps.
Irishmen celebrate this day in ev'ry clime,
Though you came from th' Shannon, th' Suir, or th' Boyne.
Remember your country, though in foreign lands ;
Whether you came from th' Blackwater, Slaney, or Bann ;
Though you came from th' Nore, th' Barrow, or Dee ;
The Bride, th' Liffey, Deel, Moy, or the Lee—
From th' Kerry Reeks to th' mountains of Down,
Mount Nephin, Barthowra, Slievenamon th' renown'd,
Slieve Bloom, Arra, Keeper, and Mount Leinster ;
Mangerton, Commeragh, and Howth, near th' Liffey.
Remember your mission your country to free,
From the peaks of Slieve Guillion to th' stately Galtees.
Your tall mountaineers would all fight to-morrow,
From th' Giant's Causeway to th' hills of Duhallow ;
From th' shores of Lough Erne to th' plains of Kildare,
Th' Lakes of Killarney to th' banks of Lough Neagh ;
From th' shores of Lough Foyle, Lough Mask, or Lough
    Carra ;
From th' hill of Howth to wild Connemara.

You're all Irish, from the Bann to the Shannon ;
From Leinster, from Munster, from Ulster, Cannaught.
Remember Clontarf, where Brian vanquished th' Danes!
Forget not Tyrone and Owen, Roe, O'Neill!
Remember old Erin and her men of renown,
Sarsfield th' brave, who held Limerick town!
Remember Limerick, Blackwater, and Benburb ;
The halls of Dungannon and the Eighty-two Club.
Remember the patriots, the true and the brave ;
The heroes of Wexford in famed ninety-eight.
Irish warriors have bled from Shannon to Rhine ;
The plains of Landon and famed Fontonoy.
The United Irishmen, their fate we deplore ;
The immortal Emmet and valiant Wolf Tone.
In every clime Irishmen have shown valor,
From th' Hudson to Ganges, from Danube to Shannon.
Irish Ciceroes England's misrule long withstood,
Th' patriots O'Connell, Curran, Grattan, and Flood.
Other patriots 'gainst wrongs their pens did wield,
Meagher, Mitchel, McGee, Davis, and Shiel.
Ireland can boast of her scholars and schools,
In the days of the Christian and mystic Druids.
Ireland can boast of her brave chivalry,
Both Pagan and Christian of true hospitality.
Her zealous missionaries, in ages long passed,
Carried to foreign climes th' gospel and cross.
Erin, dear Erin! you're now in the shade,
The land of the warrior, the bard, and th' saint.
Be United Irishmen in heart and in name,
Though your sires of yore came from 'yond th' Main.
Join hands and hearts with th' valiant old Gael,
You sons of the Norman, th' Saxon and Dane ;
Your sires of yore caused Erin to weep,
Ours be the mission dear Erin to free ! !

THE FALL

TURKISH AND BRITISH EMPIRES.

This is an often repeated adage,
"Scratch a Russian, I'll show you a Tartar"—
Russian, Cossack, Tartar, are the same,
Czar Peter, Genghis Khan and Tamerlane.
Many a bloody battle was carried on
Between the Tartars and the Ottoman.
Tartars and Turks will fight their battles o'er,
The Russians will take Constantinople ;
Whether Russ or Turk be victor—all the same,
If we get England into the flame.
Many a time some Irishmen have said,
England will keep from the battle's blaze.
With all her wisdom, mean tricks and saws,
She cannot resist God's own just Laws.
Ancient nations had their rise and fall ;
Oh, England ! the " writing is on the wall."
Divine prophets—wise, good, true and old,
Predict that to Palestine th' Jews'll be restored ;
Those who doubt not in divine holy writ,
Know that the Turkish empire will soon end.

The Russians then will enter Samarcand,
And next they will enter Hindostan—
The nation's flags will be unfurled—
England's navy into ruin will be hurled.
The news will resound from pole to pole
That Britannia's empire is no more !
Oh, Erin's son, thou art not forgot,
Emmet's epitaph is writ at last !
Heed you this moral, all true Irishmen,
Believe in prophecy and Columbkille ;
Let the watch-word now and ever be,
That all nations must and shall be free !

The Sweetest Here Below.

Sweet is Aurora's bright car ;
Sweet is the morning and ev'ning star ;
Sweet is th' heaven's azure blue ;
Sweet is the rainbow's vari'd hue ;
Sweet is th' moon's silvery light,
And million stars that shine by night.
Sweet is the comet's fiery train,
Th' Great Creator's power proclaims.
Sweet is th' sun's silvery sheen ;
Sweet is Flora's robe of green ;
Sweet is the light from God above,
Th' Mighty One, the Truth, the Love.

It's sweet to spend a sweet hour,
Midst blooming blossoms—vernal flowers ;
Oh, sweet is the breeze of morn,
The lark's carol, th' hunter's horn ;
And sweet is the summer breeze,
Midst peach, palm, and orange trees.
In Autumn, it is sweet to see
Luscious fruit and golden wheat ;
And winter has its delight,
With a pleasant and good wife.

It's sweet to stand on a rock—
To see th' billows roll and dash.
Sweet to sail on th' stormy main,
To see th' fishes sport and play.
It's sweet oft to be alone,
O'er mountains and glens to roam ;
O'er mountains wild and airy
To climb th' rocks to th' eagle's erie ;
Sweet to roam o'er glens enchant'd,
By fauns, sprites, and fairies haunt'd.
Sweet to roam over lonely glens,
To sit by cool and silvery rills.

Sweet to roam o'er fields and woods ;
Sweet are th' notes of singing birds ;
Sweet is th' sunset's golden hue ;
Sweet the sparkling drops of dew ;
Sweet is all of God's creation,
Give him praise and admiration !
Sweet to converse with a friend,
And in union thoughts to blend.
What dear friend can be so kind
As a sweet and loving wife !
Th' sweetest, dearest here below,
Is my belov'd —— —— -——.

Th' great secret of a happy wedd'd life,
Is to give your confidence to your wife.
Tell her your hope and aspiration,
And she'll promote your expectation.
Give her your confidence and caress,
Like a babe upon its mother's breast.

——, ——, my dear, my love, before you sleep,
Send to th' Good God a prayer for me ;
And in the morning when you awake,
Oh, pray for me—oh, do for God's sake.

Pray that God may crown me with success,
And that my labors may be blessed ;
That God may give you to me for a wife,
To love and comfort me in this life ;
And when we leave this world o' vexation,
That God may crown us with salvation.
———, ——, my lovely dear, and sweet pet,
In my prayers, I'll ne'er you forget ;
Sweetest, purest, loveliest, precious dear,
"Merry Christmas and a happy New Year."

Do not, my love, heed what others tell you ;
You'll find me loving, honorable and true.
Oh, ———, ——, this doubt would soon depart,
If you'd know the purity of my heart!
Sweetest, dearest, loveliest, precious dove,
Oh, have you ever felt the pangs of love?
———, have you felt love's burning pain?
Then heed my plaintive and sorrowful tale.
Will you, dear, excuse this poetic strain ?
It relieves my heart of grief and pain!!
Oh, ———, ——, ———, oh, for the time
When I can call you my sainted wife !
God bless you, dear, now and hereafter,
And your sweet niece and lovely daughters.
Your true lover, now and forevermore,
Yours, in love and friendship, ——, ———.

'HE FALL OF THE TURKISH EMPIRE.

———•+•———

\

THE crescent banner long in triumph waved
O'er the Turkish pirate and the Christian slave :
Greece, the land of science, arms and arts,
Thy sons were sold as slaves in Turkish marts.
In Turkish slave marts often were seen
For sale, like cattle, the noble Greeks,
Whose sires, in the days of Grecian renown,
Ancient civilization handed down.
Moslem warriors, with sword in hand,
Spread desolation o'er sea and land.
Those fierce fanatics, fired with zeal,
O'erthrew Jerusalem—enslav'd the Greeks.
Yea, Christian captives from every land,
With the heathen were sold in Turkish marts.
Turkish pirates roam'd o'er every main,
To furnish Turkey with Christian slaves.
Franks, Italians, Greeks, were sold by caitiffs
As slaves, to fierce and lusty califs.
The Turks' rallying cry in every battle,
"There is but one God—Mahomet is Prophet.
Slay thine enemies—take their goods and life—
Your reward is Heaven or Paradise."
Oh, Jerusalem, what a foul disgrace !

Omar, with "dirty sheep skins," sat in th' holy place.
The Moslem barbarians, in their wild zeal,
Gave libraries to the devouring flames.
The semi-barbarians thought th' prophet wise
For allowing the faithful plural wives.
Th' Mussulman fanatics, with sword in hand,
Spread Mahomet's religion o'er sea and land.
Unbelievers had no other election
But tribute, extermination, or conversion.
The Moslem tyrants all Europe did alarm
With their pirates, slave marts, and their harems.
The Turkish warriors *the world* did alarm,
Rome was saved by a tempestuous storm.
The world trembled before the Moslem van ;
At Leponta they were defeated by Don John.
All nations yielded before their advance,
Till defeated by the martial sons of France.
Two million Christians met a bloody fate
While wresting from the Moslem th' Savior's grave.
For two hundred years of bloody strife
Fought many a Christian chief and noble knight.
They fought for Christ, religion, fame, and renown,
Civilization, liberty, and the martyr's crown.
Their degenerate sons, alas! for shame,
Cry o'er the cross let the crescent wave!
Oh, it's strange—it's wicked and absurd,
To see so many Christians turn Turks!
O, mammon, to fill commercial marts,
Degenerate Christians wave th' crescent o'er the cross!
Does it not move a Christian's heart to ire,
When reading of Bulgarian villages on fire?
Oh, how women and children shriek'd and groan'd,
Before the Bashi Bazouks fire and sword!
The Turkish crescent is on the wane ;
The Ottoman empire is doomed by fate ;

The Turkish power will have a fall ;
The fatal writing is on the wall ;
The news will resound from pole to pole
That the Turkish empire is no more.
On Sophia's th' cross 'ill be unfurled,
Constantinople (——) mistress of the world ! !

PRESIDENT HAYES,

A SATIRE.

Grant's conspiracy was a military display—
An intimidation to inaugurate Hayes—
Many Democrats who want'd a legal decision,
Joined Republicans for an Electoral Commission.
Many Democrats, as in days of yore,
Put faith in th' Judges of the Supreme Court—
The Republicans managed the wires ;
They got three of the Judges out of the five.
The three Judges though well versed in lore,
Cared little for law, honor, or oaths.
Miller, Strong, and Bradley—well learn'd in law—
Would'nt investigate perjury, forgery, fraud.
Bradley said there wasn't law 'gain fraud or deceit—
The logic of th' *Serpent* that tempted Eve.
The people no longer the Courts did admire,
And the Supreme Court then sunk in the mire!
When th' decision of th' Commissioners was known,
That th' majority behind th' returns wouldn't go,
Many Democrats did then rave and bluster—
They thought to keep out Hayes by filibuster.
Then Foster, a wily and sly old knave,
Promised th' "*Governors*" for votes for Hayes,

Matthews and Foster—Hayes' abettors—
By such means made a fraudulent President.
The old abolitionists were sorely startled
By Hayes' inaugural and Southern policy.
Th' fraudulent President to condone his sins,
Put into his Cabinet some wornout Whigs.
To cover up the theft of a political dastard,
Hayes put into his Cabinet some so-called Democrats.
They were professed Democrats—Democrats to win—
With them he thought to resurrect the fossil Whigs.
The fraudulent President—oh! Tylerism—
Tried to break up his party for Whigism.
To carry out the bargain, as hinted before,
Hayes sent to Louisiana a Commission of "one-to-four."
They had their instructions from Billy Evarts—
"Buy up Packard"—"Don't investigate th' election."
The Louisiana question was a hard nut to crack.
Some one once exclaimed, "Write me down an ass"—
No matter what poet from Chaucer to Tupper—
Hayes recognized Nichols—Hayes th' usurper.
It needs no logic, it is only too plain,
If Packard wasn't elected, neither was Hayes—
Time reveals secrets of time and States.
It will yet prove a bargain and sale.
Grant left a nut to crack for Rutherford Hayes,
To manage th' "color line" in the duplicate States.
This was an anomaly never seen before—
Duplicate Governors, Legislatures, and Courts.
Many Republicans became alarmed
At Hayes' attempt to break up their party—
The Whigs hoisted on their banner of party,
The motto, "Currency," "Improvement," "Tariff."

Before election, Hayes cried "civil reform,"
Rotten Treasury, Boutwell, Richardson, alarm.

To defraud Tilden was a very mean thing,
His majority was a million white men.
Key to the Democrats, said join th' Whig line.
"You'll get a part of th' Federal spoils"—
Th' President *de facto*, Rutherford Hayes,
Made a Senator in the Buckeye State—
His letter to Garfield was a whopper—
To yield the field to Stanley Matthews.
He said my influence will, I've no doubt,
Make you the Speaker of the next House.
Democrats have a majority true,
But you'll see what my influence will do.
Oh, what shameful corrupt bargain and sale—
A political reward to th' agent of Hayes!
Before election, the cry of Jim Blaine,
Was, beware of Tilden and Southern claims—
What a shock it was for President Hayes,
His repudiation by the Buckeye State—
On the Fourth of July, Independence Day.
Hayes was denounced publicly by Jim Blaine,
Who opened his oratorical battery,
And denounced Hayes and his Mexican policy.
Hayes promis'd reform in the civil service,
While spending campaign funds in the election.
But the campaign money was not from his bank,
But the wages of postmasters and Federal clerks.
Hayes' administration is a sad miscarriage,
An illegitimate child legaliz'd by marriage!

1878.

The cry of the shylocks and the banks,
Was give us specie—gold-bearing bonds—
They would rob the cradle and the dead
For gold-bearing bonds and "poun l of flesh;"

But the face of the bonds would not do,
With the flesh they would have the blood too.
Hayes to please the bondholder's gold ring,
In seventy-eight veto'd th' Silver Bill.
He spoke of sacred contracts and law—
Oh, thou hypocrite, thou fraud of frauds—
Fraudulent President, what a fall,
Anderson guilty of forgery, fraud.
Judge Manning winked at rascality—
Anderson was released by technicality—
Th' Attorney Gen'ral mov'd for a new trial,
But the Supreme Court would not stand fire.
Hayes kept in office Returning Board hacks.
In Louisiana, their deputies and clerks—
To shut up the mouth of a tool (—) dastard.
He made a British Consul of Packard,
Who was well paid (—) his agent and tool,
In the commercial city o' Liverpool.
Thou fraudulent President what pain,
It brought thy heart—th' investigation by Blair—
To oust the President from station
By th' Supreme Court investigation.
Florida and Louisiana grief did bring
By the disclosures of Weber and McLin,
To drive fraudulent Hayes from his station
Inspired Congressional investigation—
Seventy-eight, on th' thirteenth day of May,
In Congress th' Democrats met in array—
Th' Republican tactics was time and bluster
To prevent a quorum by filibuster—
Hayes and his friends all over the nation
Tried to prevent an investigation—
Hayes didn't like Democratic attitude.
He spoke with rage of Southern ingratitude.
Hayes says there is n't a remedy in law,

To oust a President chosen by fraud.
Hayes said Tilden might ask a *quo warranto*,
But that the Supreme Court would say, ' 'No, no.''
Hayes men rail'd at investigation—
They say it 'll ruin business relation—
If political frauds are n't defeated,
Again, and again they 'll be repeated.
The Hayes men are for force and fraud still,
From the Treasury their pockets they fill.
The politicians eat th' people's bread,
They'd rob the grave, the living, and the dead.
If we sanction usurpation and fraud—
They will ov'rthrow th' Constitution and th' law.
If we don't stand by the Constitution,
We 'll have anarchy and revolution.
Hayes wants a standing army, of course,
To uphold usurpation by force.
Hayes 'd prefer war and desolation,
Rather than lose his usurp'd station.
Hayes men feel the lash of Butler Ben—
They fear they 'll lose the Treasury bin.
Ben Butler leaves th' Republican raft,
As ra's leave a rotten ship or craft.
For Butler knows of what he's thinking,
For the Republican craft is sinking.
Key's lettler to th' South is understood,
As a threat of civil war and blood.
Hayes fears Potter's investigation,
A dead lock—"non-coöperation."
He fears caucuses and like agreement,
He fears removal by impeachment.
Hayes' men fear the light of detection,
For their overthrow of free election.
Hayes men sneer and snarl at Pottery,
They fear he will smash Hayes' crockery,

Then we will hear no more mockery.
But fierce abuse of democracy,
Sherman is mad, he 'll not get better,
From th' attack of "Anderson letter"—
Sherman, Matthews, Hayes (——) oh, what alarm!
Anderson not sent to a climate warm—
On a voyage, on a long, long trip,
To Pluto's kingdom for a consulship.
Th' fraudulent President could hide sin,
By sending Anderson to Tientsin.
Treasury Sherman, your wealth is great ;
You know how to manage the syndicate.
Well you know how your pockets to fill,
For you can draw water to your mill.
Hayes, Sherman, Matthews, Harlan, did wilt
When it was known their knowledge of guilt—
Th' guilt o' corruption, forgery, and fraud—
The violation o' oaths, honor, and law—
Th' guilt of fraud, forgery, deception
In the presidential election.
To Hayes it brought dishonor, grief, woe,
For not sending McLin to Mexico.
A halter on his neck he would slip,
Rather than he'd give him a Judgeship!
Hayes' and Sherman's characters doth sink ;
They cannot be saved by Mrs. Jenks!
Stanley Matthews, thou art a mere tool!
Thou art a coward! thou art a fool!
Why did you shrink from investigation,
To keep a usurper in his station?
Dio Lewis the workingmen would feed,
While working hard, on "two cents' worth o' beef."
Lewis and th' monopolists have cheek ;
They'd have men live on fifty cents a week.
This is all nonsense, and mere claptrap,

From third-rate lecturers, fools, and quacks.
Grant men want war and blood—civil strife—
An army to shoot workingmen on the strike.
Th' men who marched with Grant with knapsacks,
When they ask for work, are called tramps.
Grant wants an army, like other nations,
Monarchy, blood, and usurpation.
Jay Gould monopolists and th' gold ring
Are now asking for Grant as a king.
Remember the fable of the frogs,
Jupiter, Apollo, and King Log.
God save the Republic from the shock,
And from the destruction of King Stork.
The soldiers' vote Gen'ral Grant will kill,
Because he veto'd their bounty bill!
Shylocks, bondholders, and corrupt rings
Sent Grant to Europe to train as king.
Grant apes the manners of th' kingly school;
He'd like to be a lord or a grand duke.
His great ambition soars higher still—
President, dictator, and then king!
Politicians want to get Grant back,
And trot him on the presidential track.
The monopolist and th' whiskey ring
Want Grant as dictator or a king.
Th' cry of strong government (——), monarchy,
Is raised by th' codfish aristocracy.
Who are the purse-proud aristocracy?
Those who get wealth by rascality.
A thing for jeers, sneers, and mockery,
Is American aristocracy!
Monopolists, rings (——), shoddyocracy,
Will make th' country a Plutocracy.
If monopolists and th' whiskey ring
Make Grant a dictator or a king,

He'll drive the country to revolution,
Which 'll end in despotism and dissolution!
The cry is raised of "tramp! tramp!"
To make a president-king of Grant.
God save the country from such a thing
As Grant for president (——), tyrant, king!
The monopolists and purse-proud snobs
Call the poor workingmen commune tramps.
The Shylocks—bondholders—will th' day rue
That they drew the line between th' rich and poor.
Where would be the rich man's store of pelf
But for th' poor man's sweat (——), th' source of all
    wealth?
Snobs, monopolists, and their tools (——), knaves—
Cannot make white Americans slaves.
Let the shout resound from sea to sea,
That the people must and shall be free!
We'll not listen to such silly things,
Th' right divine of bondholders and kings.
Purse-proud snobs lisp the new-coined slang,
And brand good poor men as commune tramps.
The workingmen without fear or dread
Must and shall have their rights—work or bread!
The people read (——), rich man, understand,
You can't enslave the people by "tramp! tramp!"
Th' rich man cries (——), "I care not, right or wrong;
'We must have a government that's strong."
Oh, remember Freedom leads the van;
Tyranny yields to th' "divine right of man!"
If Wealth should try Liberty to inthrall,
Wealth, not Liberty, must in the conflict fall.
Th' bankers' wealth is in bonds and notes of hand;
In revolutions it would slip like sand.
It's th' experience of man in ev'ry age and clime,
That the source of wealth is from land, sea, and mine.

Hark ye! hark ye! ye Shylocks and sharks :
The people's march—tramp, tramp, tramp !
Behold the people marching up in force,
Where all have equal rights, to the polls.
At the polls th' people will take their stand,
And in their might vote down the bogus banks.
We'll have, as in Jackson's time of yore,
A nation's currency—treasury notes.
The Shylocks who in bonds put their trust,
Th' revolution will their bubble burst.
The workingmen 'll seek retribution
In the forthcoming revolution.
O Shylock! Shylock! the time is ripe
For the people to assert their rights.
Fear you (——) th' terrific and awful strife,
Th' people's struggle for bread and life.
Hark ye, hark ye, Shylocks! hark with dread !
The people's grand march for work and bread !
Oh, you who would save this nation's life,
Don't drive workingmen into a strike !
Remember, remember, foolish snobs,
That your own dear offspring may yet tramp !
Remember, mothers, your darling child —
Can you tell where he will end his life ?
You who oppress workingmen (——) quite sore,
Remember that Christ was of the poor.
That person does deserve a halter
Who'd feed men only on bread and water.
Workingmen, heed not th' money-kings' tune
Of tramp, tramp, tramp—commune, commune !
Th' cry of " commune, tramp, tramp, tramp ! "
Is raised by the bondholding clan.
The cry of workingmen for work and food,
Will not be hushed by " commune ! commune ! "

1879.

New England fishermen, in days o' yore,
Fished in the sea, and along th' shore.
* Those poor fishermen were brave and free ;
They fought tyrants both by land and sea ;
They fought for freedom and human rights ;
They nobly bled under th' stars and stripes.
England came with a piratic band,
She claim'd dominion by sea and land.
She said, Samuel, this is my wish,
That you pay millions for my fish.
Samuel, another word with thee,
I'll sell my fish in thy markets free.
Evarts, you put your fish to your nose,
And I'll walk off with this bag of gold.
The people yet will let England see,
That the ocean must and shall be free ;
Free from pole to pole, from clime to clime,
Then fishermen can cast net and line.
In their utter despair, Hayes men sought,
To shield fraud with telegrams in naught ;
Officeholders and "penny-a-liners,"
Would shield Hayes by telegrams in cipher.
Before th' Potter investigation,
Gov. Tilden made this revelation—
He swore on his honor and solemn oath,
That in the South he never bought a vote.
That in Louisiana votes were for sale,
That he ne'er bid or bargained for th' same.
Republicans must now stop their scoffing,
Telegrams in cipher are naught—nothing.
And although Hayes holds his usurped place,
Tilden was elect'd President—all th' same.
A greater curse than war, famine, plague,

Is the treaty made by Burlingame.
By that treaty the Mongolian race,
Like clouds of locusts, our free shores invade.
The Chinese heathens believe not in God,
They adore wood and stone (——) the idol.
If we don't stop Chinese immigation,
With leprosy they 'll infect the nation ! !
The workingmen will find out too late,
That Chinamen have made them mere slaves.
The workingmen must have meat and bread,
And their wives and children must be fed.
John Chinaman lives (——) on a groat (Grwat),
Carrion, vermin, rice, mice, cat, and rat.
We must stop Mongolian immigration,
Or it 'll blast Caucasian civilization ! !
No more heathens from Empire Ta Tsing,
Was the text of th' anti-Chinese bill.
Import no more than fifteen at a time—
The penalty one hundred dollars fine.
Monopolists swore that they 'd be Hayes' foe,
Unless the Chinese bill he would veto.
The President, the offspring of fraud,
On the veto for awhile did halt.
This was sham, a political trick,
For with the rich did n't he always stick.
Hayes would make all white men human chattel,
Rather than merchants 'd lose Chinese cattle.
The fraud spoke of treaty denunciation,
Who trampled on sacred obligation !.
He said all right, th' denunciation
Of the treaty with " La Great Nation."
The French fought England by land and sea,
To make America great and free.
What base ingratitude for French valor—
Preference for heathens and their dollar.

The great fraud gave Congress a snubbing ;
Those who install'd 'im deserv'd a drubbing.
Hayes would deprive freemen of their birthright,
He's a Federalist of the bluest light.
Treaties are n't binding in time of danger,
From pestilence, war (——) or the invader.
Th' invasion of Mongolians and Tartars,
Eclipse (——) Huns, Goths, and Vandals.
A nation's life and self-preservation,
Is a higher law than obligation ! !
Working men, remember Hayes with a will,
And his veto of th' anti-Chinese bill !
Beecher's preaching is all gammon ;
For his great idol is mammon.
Indeed, his motives are all for self,
Pleasure, mammon, the world and the flesh.
Beecher's object is, the rich to please,
He's the champion of leprous Chinese.
He'd import a Chinese human flood ;
He would make white men hewers of wood.
He wants hordes of leprous yellow races,
To bring white men to starvation wages.
Bondholders, bankers, usurious knaves,
With specie payment th' people now enslave.
The shylocks cry rag-baby and rags—
From th' revenue they fill their money bags.
The people 'll rally from shore to shore,
Against th' banks as Jackson did of yore.
Bondholders, on their way to heaven,
Are Christians one day out of seven.
But on the other six days mammon's crew
Are extortionists, sharpers, shavers—Jew.
This once glorious and great nation,
Is now enslaved by taxation.
Th' people 're tax'd from an anchor to a nail,

And from a match e'en to the ships that sail.
When a party is long in power,
It becomes corrupt, rotten, and foul.
The people will, for they are able,
Clean out the political stable.
And all corrupt, rotten, and foul filth,
With its corrupt party send adrift.
Long the people will be great and free,
If they only vote 'gainst the " term three."
This country will fall like other nations,
If parties are kept too long in stations.
Long the people will avert their doom,
If they read the fall of Greece and Rome—
Bribes, ambition, luxury, and wealth,
In Greece and Rome o'erthrew th' commonwealth.
Its the destiny, the fate of all,
Empires and Republics (——) rise and fall.
Greece and Italy were great and grand,
One a speck, and t'other a strip of land.
These famed countries, once were great and free,
They held dominion by land and sea.
Their men were wise—their warriors great,
They vanquished realms and many a State.
Glory—martial flame, their soldier hearts did fire,
They thought it sweet for their country to expire.
But sad the change, and sad, indeed, the theme,
They became slaves, who once were brave and free.
Love of country disappeared by stealth,
Thro' bribes, poverty, luxury, and wealth.
The rich men influenced the masses,
They drew a line between the classes.
Th' invaders came—th' common scourge of all,
Ah, both rich and poor they did inthrall.
Americans, what e'er be your stations,
Remember the fate of other nations.

Columbia once was brave and free,
Now th' country's corrupt from sea to sea!
At elections men are bought and sold,
With office, greenbacks, silver, and gold.
Who sells his vote is a human chattel,
The rich buy him as they do their cattle!
The franchise is more precious than fine gold,
Too precious either to be bought or sold.
Let the people now a law devise,
Buyer and seller to disfranchise!
Now we must stop corruption's rapid tide,
Or th' country 'll be rotten ere it 'll be ripe.
Political rings don't think it funny,
That satirists have more gall than honey.
Politicians dread my predictions,
As they fear my maledictions.
Vile politicians now feel my satire,
Dunces won't sneer at it, and think for awhile.
Corrupt politicians dread my ire,
Justice, humor, truth, wit, sarcasm, satire.
Grant loves the chime of the Chinese gong,
And he wants heathen hordes from Hong Kong.
Grant speaks with wrath of demagogism,
He wants to establish Cæsarism.
What a curse awaits Caucasian breed,
If it be mixed with inferior seed.
Ah, the curse—the fall—what degradation,
Awaits the crime of amalgamation.
Ah, behold with horror and with dread,
That feeble offspring of th' white and red.
Does it improve the noble Caucasian stock,
The tawny offspring of the white and black?
Oh, degraded offspring of the white man,
Mixture of black, red, yellow, brown, and tan.
Horrid goblin—monster—what e'er you be;

Hideous creature, how long will you be free?
Woe, woe,—abomination!
—— Grant and Chinese immigration!!
Grant was foolish—he was not witty—
He ask'd a reception from Cork city—
Drinking with lords, dukes, and princes, what not,
He became stupid—he became a sot.
From eating and drinking—whisky—beer,
He forgot the Centennial year,
When Ireland sent o'er a delegation,
With an address from the Irish nation.
Grant was President—in high station ;
He said there was no " Irish nation ! ! "
Grant may now pick his teeth with a fork,
He 'll n't get a blarney-dinner from Cork.
Arise, thou prophet, bard, saint, and sage,
Denounce the sins of this venal age.
And you, who in the pulpit (——) stand,
Denounce the corruption of the land!
And denounce the rulers of the nation,
For bribery—stealing—peculation !
And denounce th' "pharisaical" faces,
Of all who steal in high and low places.
And denounce all mean, corrupt ringers,
As vile, pollut'd, and wicked sinners.
Denounce as hideous, vile, and loath,
The wretch who buys or sells a vote!
May God touch your lips with holy fire,
And may he fill your hearts with his ire.
May he give you strength to take a stand,
For to scourge corruption from the land!
Why sit'st thou there with limbs of sloth,
Wrapt in sable or ermine robes.
Oh, thou wert once a man beheld with awe,
An expounder—an oracle of law —

For to shield the weak against the strong,
To maintain the right, to punish wrong,
And a shield against intrusion—
——— expounder of th' Constitution.
You've made th' Constitution a thing of wax,
To rob the people with a " bonus " tax.
For the Supreme Courts of the nation
Have enslav'd th' people with taxation.
So away with humbug and clap-trap,
Now I'll let you know what I am at—
That the Supreme Courts of the nation
Have aided railroad corporations,
Even by (———) one majority,
To confiscate private property.
Constitutional law is lax—
Th' courts put on a railroad " bonus " tax.
By the courts, let it be understood—
——— to rob th' people is n't for th' public good.
To pile the wealth of the whole nation
In the hands of railroad corporations,
To the people it matters not a straw—
Their money is gone by tricksters or th' law.
Bards and wits, in ages long, long past,
On the stage, crimes and tyrants did lash ;
They feared not th' despot's frown and ire,
They lashed his crimes with keen satire.
Against corruption they spoke and writ,
Kings quail'd before their humorous wit.
Th' crimes and follies of a venal age,
Were the jest and laughter of the stage.
The crimes of kings were shown in tragedy,
The crimes of knaves were shown in comedy.
Tragedian, comedian (———) the buffoon,
Genius, sarcasm, satire, and lampoon,
Wit and humor—such (———) as these,

Knaves and monarchs alike did tease.
All you, who write or who act on the stage,
Denounce th' crimes and corruption of the age!!
Denounce political dishonesty,
Federal, State, and municipality!!

The true genius, the despot's hand won't kiss,
Nor cares he whether mobs or reptiles hiss.
He cares not whether fools or despots blame,
His great object is, an immortal name!
Italia's bard on his foes pour'd ire,
Like Vesuvius' volcanic fire.
Against his foes satire was hurled—
His poems are th' wonder of the world.
Satirists, in ev'ry age and nation,
From oppression have drawn inspiration.
Poets are inspir'd by the powers above,
Their great inspiration is from hate and love.
Th' lays of other bards our hearts do move,
With their strains of unrequited love.
The bards Camoens, Petrarch, and Tasso,
Their fate was disappointment, grief, and woe.
Oft genius is sorely distressed,
While fools and knaves with wealth are possessed.
Poets oft have felt penury's fierce dart,
For they would not practice the courtly art ;
The art to flatter and to fawn
On royalty's mean reptile spawn.
Satirist often write to punish wrong,
Love often inspires a verse or a song.
To save his life from a briny grave,
Camoens swam on the ocean's wave.
He saved his poem—what joy—pleasure,
Though the wreck went down with his treasure.
The great poet, with one hand buffeted th' waves,

And with th' other his great poem did save.
In this world of disappointment and strife,
An author loves his own book more than life ;
Racked with care, an author's heart we find,
For the fate of the child of his mind.
His heart trembles between hope and despair,
"None but an author knows an author's care."
His thoughts have life—they are a living soul ;
Unborn millions oft they do control.
His anxious care is from last to first,
That his thoughts should not perish with his dust.
Whether he be rich or poor, lame or blind,
His great thoughts will live with men of mind.
An author's spirit oft roams o'er and o'er
Empires, kingdoms, islands, seas, and shore.
An author's spirit often wings its flight
To God's throne, and 'yond the limit of light.
His spirit roams through space until at last
Other universes are reached and passed.
Onward, onward, his thoughts are so fleet
That they reach th' secrets of th' utmost deep.
His thoughts will move onward until yet
This universe will appear a speck !
Science great secrets will yet disclose,
Th' telescope 'll multiply a billion fold.
How grand the heavens—oh, how sublime,
Its million suns in great splendor shine—
Th' milky way paved with suns so bright—
Suns of splendor and varied light.
And through optic glasses will yet be seen,
Suns red, purple, orange, yellow, and green.
And their beauties will be unfurled,
With comets, planets, and many worlds.
Th' moon 'll be a near neighbor—nearer still
Than a church on a neighboring hill.

And if in the moon are living people,
They 'll appear like men on a steeple.
Th' bard—historian, though often sad,
—— disappointment will not make him mad.
From nature he draws an inspiration ;
From the world's follies a detestation.
He beholds nature's treasures—how grand
The starry heavens—sea and land.
He cares not for monarchs, princes, or powers,
He sees more splendor in a thousand flowers.
Though poor in purse, he enjoys pleasure
From God's inexhaustable treasure.
He sees great men into exile driven ;
He sees scepters, crowns, and empires riven.
—— th' fleeting pleasures of this sublunar vale.
For all, all perish—are they not all frail ?
The world's pomp and wealth are all vanity,
—— th' miser's passion is all insanity.
The miser's grasp for gold ceases never,
As if he'd live ever and forever.
For to gain wealth, millions become knaves,
And millions more self-imposed slaves.
Ah, for the world's perishable treasure,
They lose health, God's love, and nature's pleasure.
What sleepless nights—what feverish care,
To amass wealth for a spendthrift heir.
And the wealth one generation doth gather,
A second and third dissipate and scatter !
In toil and moil many a life is spent
To obtain wealth which brings but discontent.
Many a heart is sorely oppressed,
Tho' diamonds glitter on th' noxious breast.
They sigh for love and happiness in vain,
They worship their idol—power and gain.
Happy th' hermit in other days and climes,

Who renounced the world—its pomp and pride.
Thrice more happy the savage and barbarian,
Than labor oppress'd by civilization!
The greatest curses of civilization,
Are credit, interest, and taxation!
Sad comfort—to rot in rose-wood coffin—
You who robb'd the widow and the orphan.
The widow's curse and the orphan's tears
Will haunt your poor soul in after years.
Oh, the moans, the groans, the shriek, and yell,
When the damned soul first enters hell!
Th' bard—historian, in his heart is sad,
He sees that millions, in this world are mad.
Dunces may say he is proud, vain—
—— They know not what makes his heart so glad.
Old nature affords him joy and pleasure,
Even chaos yields him hidden treasure.
He beholds secrets, as with eyes of light,
In the womb of nature, chaos, and old night.
He communes with worlds and beings so bright,
That they dim the sun, moon, and stars of light.
The psalmist pour'd his thoughts sublime
Midst flocks and fields, and o'er Palestine.
Th' bard with satire pierces the vile defamer,
Th' quack, th' bigot, and political schemer.
The winter of life is sad and dreary,
With a poet it's all summer—dreamy.
By the world's care his heart oft is stung,
Yet his hopes do bloom, his heart is young.
His thoughts are noble, sublime, and grand,
He makes his home in a fairy land.
He sees disappear many nationality,
Republics, empires, and many a dynasty.
Great cities—many a commercial mart,
With mammon's votaries—are now forgot.

Fearless the eagle sweeps o'er Alpine crags,
And the condor o'er Chimborazo's rocks,
And on their flights midst perpetual snow,
Behold kings and slaves on the plains below.
So an author looks down from on high,
And for Adam's offspring breaks a sigh.
From his lofty plain he is a judge,
O'er potentates, powers, and the drudge.
He beholds millions to slavery doomed ;
And countless tyrants in dust entombed ;
And human mortals, the world's disgrace,
Without a tomb—now a nameless race—
And gorgeous temples, palaces, and shrines,
He sees crumble by the tooth of time ;
And systems, the world's fear and wonder,
Like great thunder-clouds rent asunder ;
And systems that have made man a slave,
In time 'll perish save only the name.
Hope often to an author's heart doth send,
Th' thought that he has a thousand thousand friends,
That's balm to his heart, in his wearied strife—
Conflict—and on the journey of life !
Oh, forward, forward is the march of the mind,
It 'll leave ignorance and bigotry behind.
Tremble, you despots and bigots again,
Dread you the weapon—the press and the pen.
Fear not the truth whoever you may be,
For the truth will make you ever free.
Why do so many tremble and quail,
If they believe that truth will prevail ?
Why do they fear truth's investigation ;
For truth will not bar their salvation ?
Why this great alarm and this affright ;
Fear not knowledge and truth's holy light ?
That system that would truth inthrall,

Let that system in the conflict fall.
Realms will perish—perish mammon's gain,
Ever and ever truth will prevail.
Systems that man worship and cherish,
If false to truth in time shall perish.
Millions are lost by war and starvation,
By a false modern civilization.
This boasted civilization is a fraud,
A violation of God's and nature's laws.
To fight for tyrants, millions are doomed—
In gloomy mines millions are entombed.
Millions work for scant food and to pay rent,
That th' rich may have millions—their lives are spent.
The workingmen, with a brow of care,
Make the wealth which they can never share.
Civilization millions has driven,
To toil in factories—to pine in prison.
Civilization is best—best understood,
When it makes men happy—its for the public good.
That a few rich men do millions plunder,
Is n't th' greatest good to the greatest number.
Great cities are political sores,
The scenes of vice, ignorance, and woe.
You, who try to convert foreign peoples,
See vice under th' shadow of your steeples.
Behold th' shouts of a clamorous throng,
For a party either right or wrong.
Men oft are politically insane,
They lose principle, but cling to a name!
The President assumes dignity,
To hide partisan malignity.
The bill for free elections, so, so,
Fraudulent Hayes did quash with his veto.
High, indeed, is the President's station,
When he vetoes the voice of the nation.

We have fallen on an evil hour,
If we surrender to th' *one man power.*
Hayes wants th' army, fraud, and deception,
To control th' coming election!
American parents will come to grief,
From the opium eating heathen Chinese.
Alas! alas! your grief will begin,
Your sons 'll enter th' smoking Chinese den.
Your wealth 'll give you little satisfaction,
Your sons eat opium (——) stupefaction.
Great will be the nation's degradation!
—— opium eaters— abomination!
Th' Republic will have a downward course,
When elections are controlled by force.
Roman liberty met its doom—fall,
When rulers employ'd th' Prætorian Guard.
Alas! alas! for liberty's sad fate,
If the presidents should control the State.
The Federalists' malignity,
Wants to destroy the State's sovereignty.

Campaign Songs, 1880.

GRANT'S MARCH.

Air—*"Billy O'Rourke."*

I.

In sixty-eight, 'remind the date,
  Republicans did falter ;
They want'd a chief to save retreat,
  Defeat and a great slaughter.
They look'd about in fear and doubt,
  For a man to bear their banner ;
They found out, a tool and clout,
  In the Galena Tanner.
Hurrah ! my boys, we'll all rejoice,
  The lad is out of station,
Without a joke, he'll cut his throat,
  And God will save the nation.

II.

President Grant was so sly,
  When he got into station ;
On th' Treasury he cast an eye,
  To feed his poor relations.
At the public crib he did feed,
  With politicians and others ;
Bondholders and banking thieves,
  His father, sons and brothers.

Hurrah! my boys, we'll all rejoice,
  The lad is out of station ;
Without a joke, he'll cut his throat,
  And God will save the nation.

III.

In the South he made a rout,
  With soldiers and bayonets ;
Liberty he would stamp out,
  And th' nation he'd enslave it.
Presents, too, he got a few,
  From many thieving ringers ;
From bankers and shylock Jews,
  And " politician " sinners.
Hurrah! my boys, we'll all rejoice,
  The lad is out of station ;
Without a joke, he'll cut his throat,
  And God will save the nation.

IV.

Grant's record is very bad,
  It will not bear inspection ;
He was th' dupe of a roguish gang,
  To o'erthrow free election.
The President was a Hayes man,
  The tool of frauds and deceivers ;
With fraud, he ousted Tilden Sam,
  And put in Hayes the schemer.
Hurrah! my boys, we'll all rejoice,
  The lad is out of station ;
Without a joke, he'll cut his throat,
  And God will save the nation.

V.

Gen. Grant had a time so sweet,
　　With Cockney lasses ;
He eat bread and cheese and roast beef,
　　And quaff'd many brimming glasses.
He went o'er to the Irish shore,
　　And from Dublin to Killarney,
With punch galore MaGra Ma Astore,
　　But Cork gave him no blarney.
Hurrah ! my boys, we'll all rejoice,
　　The lad is out of station ;
Without a joke, he'll cut his throat,
　　And God will save the nation.

VI.

On the Rhine he drank good wine,
　　In Berlin he eat sausage ;
He had a ride in many a clime,
　　And Samuel paid his passage.
Of greenbacks, too, he spent a few,
　　In many a clime and station ;
The money of the bankers—Jews,
　　And the plunder of the nation.
Hurrah ! my boys, we'll all rejoice,
　　The lad is out of station ;
Without a joke, he'll cut his throat,
　　And God will save the nation.

VII.

Grant cross'd the sea ; he drank tea
　　With the heathen Chinese races ;
While on a spree, with great glee,
　　He kissed their yellow faces.

Powers above, he fell in love,
    With the pigtail Chinese lasses ;
He was like a sucking dove,
    While tippling with their glasses.
Hurrah ! my boys, we'll all rejoice,
    The lad is out of station ;
Without a joke, he'll cut his throat,
    And God will save the nation.

VIII.

The kingly school and banking Jews
    Want Grant to rule the nation ;
Bondholders and the thieving crew
    Shall ne'er put him in station.
What will he do, he's in a stew,
    The people all they hate him ;
He's in despair I do declare,
    His mind is getting crazy.
Hurrah ! my boys, we'll all rejoice,
    The lad is out of station ;
Without a joke, he'll cut his throat,
    And God will save the nation.

THE HEATHEN CHINESE.

Air—"*Groves of Blarney.*"

I.

Ye sons of freedom and working people,
    Pray give heed to my sad, dismal tale ;
It is alarming, how th' poor are starving,
    In this glorious land so fair and great.

The poor are starving, for wages are falling,
 And th' poor white man will meet a sad doom ;
In every place are Chinese crawling,
 They'll have white men's places, alas! quite soon!

II

The Chinese croakers and opium smokers,
 Like Egypt's plagues now infect the land ;
The mixed races, with yellow faces,
 The white man's labor cannot withstand.
Our gold they are hoarding to send over,
 With their dried bones to the China Sea,
While their dirty pigtails they leave forlorn,
 To breed a plague in this land once free.

III.

The heathen creatures, with loose breeches,
 Back to old China must all set sail ;
For th' country is teaming with the leeches,
 And their dirty blouses and pigtails.
The Chinese heathens now are sleeping,
 Like rats and badgers, in dens and sheds ;
The cunning people are on low feeding,
 On rice and mice, for they eat no bread.

IV.

In our laundries they are sauntering,
 In the kitchens, and in every place ;
The white people, they are alarming,
 With their pig eyes and leprous face.
Chinese heathens, from the flowery nation,
 Their immigration will have no stint,
Soon they'll have every white man's station,
 Then the white laborers may sigh and lament.

V.

A curse is awaiting this great nation,
  From th' mixed races, of inferior breed—
The abomination of amalgamation,
  With Chinese pagans, will yet proceed !
The Caucasian races will be tainted
  With inferior blood, yellow, brown and tan ;
Oh, the white faces will be painted
  With a leperous taint, from the Chinese land !

VI.

The lowest creatures and false teachers,
  The wily screechers of mammon men ;
Those false preachers, with their false speeches,
  Will make this country a Chinese den !
The Chinese pagans, in adoration,
  Kneel, in prostration, to stone and wood ;
They will blast white civilization,
  They will pour forth like a vandal flood !

VII.

Heed not the prattle of the sons of Mammon,
  For with their gammon, they'd you enslave ;
The thunder and rattle of sword and cannon,
  The poor white man must emancipate !
Heed not the Beechers, and like preachers,
  For they are screechers to be let alone ;
Follow Dennis Kearney from Killarney,
  Or from sweet Blarney Ma Cra Ma Store.

JIMMY BLAINE.

Air—*"Mary Blain."*

I.

Once there lived a saucy lad,
   Along the coast of Maine ;
Who fish'd with line and fishing rod,
   And his name was Jimmy Blaine.
     Oh, poor Jimmy Blaine,
     Oh, poor Jimmy Blaine,
     You'll ne'er'll be President
     I heard the people say.

II.

For ambition was his creed,
   And to rule the Pine Tree State :
To get great wealth was his greed,
   When Speaker he was made.
     Oh, poor Jimmy Blaine,
     Oh, poor Jimmy Blaine,
     You ne'er'll be President
     I heard the people say.

III.

Seventy-Six he took a fit,
   From which he'll not get better ;
Then he got into a sad fit
   By the Mulligan letters.
     Oh, poor Jimmy Blaine,
     Oh, poor Jimmy Blaine,
     You'll ne'er'll be President
     I heard the people say.

IV.

Blaine will be swept from power
  By the coming greenback wave ;
It will be a happy hour
  When he'll meet with his defeat.
     Oh, poor Jimmy Blaine,
     Oh, poor Jimmy Blaine,
     You'll ne'er'll be President
     I heard the people say.

V.

In Congress he proudly struts,
  For to gain power and fame ;
There he flaunts the bloody shirt,
  For it is his only game.
     Oh, poor Jimmy Blaine,
     Oh, poor Jimmy Blaine,
     You'll ne'er'll be President
     I heard the people say.

SHERMAN JOHNNY.

I.

In the Buckeye State
  Lives a man so jolly ;
He is known to fame
  As old Sherman Johnny.
     To ra lora lo, to ra lora li do.

II.

Old Sherman's wealth is very great,
 It is known to the ringers ;
He managed the Syndicate
 For bankers, Jews and sinners.
 To ra lora lo, etc.

III.

He worked early and late,
 To bring water to his miller ;
The bankers he did inflate,
 By hoarding up the silver.
 To ra lora lo, etc.

IV.

Specie he did not pay,
 People say he's brassy,
He must get out o' the way
 This old Sherman Johnny.
 To ra lora lo, etc.

V.

Oh, Sherman's character sinks,
 Oh, is it not a pity,
For he danced with Mrs. Jenks
 In New Orleans city.
 To ra lora lo, etc.

VI.

Old Sherman now doth rave,
 The bankers think him funny ;
For with their notes they shave,
 He burnt the greenback money.
 To ra lora lo, etc.

THE WORKINGMEN'S COMPLAINT.

I.

Workingmen once had good rations
　They'd plenty of mutton and beef ;
Now they're on starvation wages,
　On bread and molasses and leeks.
　　These are shocking hard times,
　　For the rich for the poor have no pity ;
　　Wages 're down in country, town and city ;
　　These are shocking hard times.

II.

The rich in Broadway do strut,
　They drink champagne by glasses ;
The poor drink water, in a hut,
　And dine on mush and molasses.
　　These are shocking hard times,
　　For the rich for the poor have no pity,
　　Wages 're down, in country, town and city ;
　　These are shocking hard times.

III.

Times were when a workingman's pay
　Was two dollars a day or more ;
He then could be merry and gay,
　He'd eating and drinking galore.
　　These are shocking hard times,
　　For the poor for the poor have no pity,
　　Wages 're down in country, town and city ;
　　These are shocking hard times.

IV.

Oh, the country will be curst,
  By Chinese immigration!
Then white men will bite the dust
  All over this great nation.
    These are shocking hard times,
    For the rich for the poor have no pity,
    Wages 're down in country, town and city ;
    These are shocking hard times.

V.

Chinese immigration must end,
  Or there'll be a war of races!
White men their rights must defend,
  Chinamen must not take their places!
    These are shocking hard times,
    For the rich for the poor have no pity,
    Wages 're down in country, town and city ;
    These are shocking hard times.

VI.

The railroads are combined
  To rob the Western farmers ;
The rich are all of a mind
  To feed men on bread and water !
    These are shocking hard times,
    For the rich for the poor have no pity,
    Wages 're down, in country, town and city ;
    These are shocking hard times.

VII.

The farmers work early and late,
  They're robbed by wheat-buying ringers,
They're taxed by county and State,
  And fleec'd by bankers and millers.

These are shocking hard times,
For the rich for the poor have no pity ;
Wages 're down, in country, town and city ;
These are shocking hard times.

DORAN'S ASS.

I.

As I was going to the Market Cross
In the highway I met Doran's Ass,
With a heavy budget on his back,
The stupid donkey lay in his tracks.
His cruel master ripped and swore,
He hammered his ass to make him go.
  If I had a donkey that would'nt go,
  Do you think I would hammer him?
      No, no, no.

II.

Poor little Franky is Doran's Ass,
On a summer's day he scamper'd off ;
This donkey ran off in the highway ;
He prick'd his ears and set up a bray ;
His cruel master ripped and swore,
He hammer'd his ass to make him go.
  If I had a donkey that would'nt go,
  Do you think I would hammer him ?
      No, no, no.

III.

On convention and election days,
Franky, the ass, for Doran doth bray ;
He is a fool—Doran's servile hack,
He carries his budget on his back.

His cruel master ripped and swore,
He hammered his ass to make him go.
If I had a donkey that wouldn't go,
Do you think I would hammer him?
No, no, no.

IV.

This stupid donkey is old and gray,
Long he was fed on the people's hay,
Th' people no longer this donkey will feed ;
He may now go to grass up Salt Creek.
His cruel master ripped and swore,
He hammer'd his ass to make him go.
If I had a donkey that would'nt go,
Do you think I would hammer him?
No, no, no.

AN EPITAPH ON DORAN'S ASS.

In th' court-house or in the highway,
Doran's old ass no more will bray ;
Remember, good people, as you pass,
That here lie the bones of Doran's Ass.

GOD MADE THE LAND FREE.

I.

Landlords and agents now may lament,
The people of Ireland'll pay them no rent ;
The people'll rally from mountain to sea,
Their houses and lands for to make free.
Ballinamona ora, Balinamona ora,
Ballinamona ora, God made the land free.

II.

Ye people of Ireland, now take a stand,
And pay no more rent, for God owns the land ;
The purse-proud lords may lament and bemoan,
But pay them no rent, for th' land is your own !
Ballinamona ora, etc.

III.

The lordly tyrants must soon have a fall,
The people no longer shall they inthrall ;
United and firm, on one thing agree,
From landlord oppression you must be free.
Ballinamona ora, etc.

IV.

God has ordained that all men who toil,
Shall ever possess the fruits of the soil ;
This is a law that God did proclaim,
That th' land is as free as th' light and th' air.
Ballinamona ora, etc.

V.

Princes and lords, with fraud and with might,
Long have usurped man's holy right ,
Despots and knaves, with th' sword and th, pen,
Have enslav'd the people again and again.
Ballinamona ora, etc.

VI.

Inscribe on your flag, in letters o' green,
That all men are born equal and free ;
From mountain and plain, march to the strife,
Fight, now and ever, for land and life.
Ballinamona ora, etc.

VII.

Oh! sing the bold anthem, from shore to shore,
That God owns the land—that God we adore ;
From landlord oppression, th' people'll be free,
They've paid for the land, they own it in fee.
    Ballinamona ora, etc.

EPIGRAM.
THE EQUALITY OF MAN.

Fear not the scorn of wealth and pride,
Or of those in lofty station ;
All men were born with equal right,
Inheritors of creation.

THE LAST FAREWELL.

I.

Hard it is to part forever,
    With the friends that we love so well ;
And from hearts so dear to sever,
    Among strangers for e'er to dwell.
With what pangs the heart is bleeding,
    Neither pen nor tongue can tell ;
We can ne'er forget that meeting,
    When we bid adieu—the last farewell.

II.

In this world of sin and sorrow,
    Let us submit to our fate ;
Pride and grief the heart doth harrow,
    When our love is paid with hate.
With silent grief the heart is breaking,
    Sad, broken hearts alone can tell,
When we fear that this sad greeting
    Will bring adieu—the last farewell.

III.

Who can tell the soul's anguish,
  When our love meets with distain,
Love from the heart we can't banish,
  Tho' the heart's sunk in despair.
The dread that from our love we'll sever,
  Binds us with a tongue-bound spell ;
Oh, that we must part forever,
  We can't say adieu—th' last farewell.

IV.

There's hope in heaven above us,
  Where all's peace with God and love,
And in heaven God will love us,
  And the Son and Spirit-Dove.
In heaven no grief doth harrow,
  For with angels we will dwell ;
We'll look back on the vale of sorrow,
  And bid the world the last farewell.

THE SADDEST THOUGHTS.

Air—"Auld Lang Syne.

I.

Sad are our thoughts when we leave home
  From a father's love and care,
And o'er this cold world to roam,
  The heart feels so sad and drear,
Sad thoughts we cannot banish,
  When we leave our mother dear ;
The soul then sinks in anguish,
  And the heart then sheds a tear.

II.

Sad are the thoughts of school-boy hours,
  And the happy days then spent ;
When we roam'd o'er fields and flowers,
  We were happy and content.
Sad are the thoughts of those bright days,
  When we knew no grief or gloom ;
Sad are the thoughts of sisters fair,
  Who now sleep within the tomb.

III.

Sad are the thoughts of former years,
  Oh, we feel them o'er and o'er.
Sad are the thoughts of brothers dear,
  And of friends we'll ne'er see more.
Sad are th' thoughts of the old fireside,
  And of friends assembled there,
When at the hour of ev'ning tide,
  We lisped a child's first prayer.

IV.

Sad are the thoughts when we lose wealth,
  Or honor, power or fame ;
Sad are the thoughts when we lose health,
  And the things we can't regain.
Sad are the thoughts of pleasures pass'd,
  Oh, they now come like a dream ;
Sad are the thoughts of what we've lost,
  And of what we might have been.

V.

Sad are th' thoughts when we depart
  From the green graves of our sires ;
With sad thoughts the soul is fraught,
  And the heart is touch'd with fire.

When those sad thoughts pierce the heart,
  Oh, the soul then knows no rest ;
Th' saddest thoughts are when we part
  With the one that we love best.

THE SWEETEST IN THE LAND.

I.

In Minnesota, lives a lady fair,
  Oh! may angels for ever guard her ;
Night and day my heart is in despair,
  For I fear I will lose my charmer ;
She's gentle and sweet, her mind is serene,
  Oh, she is both graceful and charming!
She's stately as a queen, modest and meek,
  And she blooms like the rose of morning.

II.

Fame and renown and a thousand crowns,
  And th' power of Cæsar and Alexander,
Splendor and power, I would lay down
  At the feet of Eve's fairest daughter.
Flowers in full bloom, and roses in June,
  Or Phœbus of a summer's morning ;
Sweet notes of the lute, or Orpheus' tune,
  Are n't as pleasing as my dear darling.

III.

I'd lay at her feet th' fam'd "golden fleece,"
  I'd forsake Queen Helen and Cleopatra ;
For this one so sweet, I'd forsake all Greece,
  And the daughters of famed Italia.
Blessings from above, may fall on my dove,
  Oh, of her I am nightly a dreaming ;
For with rhyme I gush, since I fell in love,
  With th' lady so beautiful and pleasing.

IV.

All the golden ore, and th' tripod of yore,
    And th' wealth of Crœsus and Great Damer,
And all the mines known on the golden shore
    I would give to this lovely fair one.
To this lady so wise, rhymes I'd indite,
    To get her for a wife I was beseeching ;
But political strife, malice and spite,
    Assailed me both noon and evening.

V.

She is fair and grand, th' sweetest in the land,
    She is as lovely as an angel ;
To get her hand, would make my soul glad,
    For in this world she has no equal.
In the stilly night, my soul sheds a tear ;
    With love for her my heart is a-sighing,
I'd lay down my life for this precious dear,
    For with grief and love I was a dying.

VI.

Once she was inclin'd to become my wife,
    Oh, how I loved and adored her,
Enemies were ripe with a thousand lies ;
    I fear she's chang'd her mind forever.
Tho' her mind be changed from love to hate,
    I hope that long years she'll be enjoying ;
I'll submit to my fate, she'll find when late,
    That my enemies all were a-lying.

EPIGRAM—TO H——.

Had I come to your house in a carriage,
    With plenty of gold and in great style ;
Ah! then had I asked you in marriage,
    Would you give me your hand with a smile?

The Darling of my Soul.

I.

On a ramble, of a summer's evening,
I met a dear creature, th' fairest to behold.
She was a lady fair, with silken flowing hair,
My heart she did insnare, which caus'd me great woe.
I'd love to meet her, and with love I'd greet her,
There's none more sweeter—the darling of my soul.

II.

This lady's most divine, she drove me to rhyme,
And the burden of my mind to her I made known—
To ease my heart, which was pierc'd with Cupid's dart,
The secret of my heart to her I did unfold.
With rhyme I did beseech her, oft did I tease her ;
But it was to please her—the darling of my soul.

III.

Oft in the stilly night my heart breaks a sigh ;
Then I shed a flood of tears, for her I adore.
This lady is so sweet, gentle and discreet ;
I fear I'll die of grief, my heart is quite sore.
When I went to see her coldly did she treat me ;
But I'd ne'er deceive her—the darling of my soul.

IV.

She is a goddess rare, none with her can compare,
My soul is in that fair, I wish she was my own.
Her I can't forget ; she's more of heaven than o' earth ;
She's fairer than Venus or Queen Helen of yore.
With love my soul is fraught, she's th' fountain of m
    thoughts ;
To gain her heart I've sought—she's th' darling of m
    soul.

V.

My love never frowns, there's a glory on her brow,
Before her I'd kneel down—she's the idol of my soul.
Could I equal Virgil's rhymes, or Homer's most sublime,
Could I touch th' Grecian lyre, my sorrow to deplore,
I'd worship this creature morning and evening ;
Oh, I'd love to please her—the darling of my soul!

VI.

Now, I'll end this rhyme, I'll love her for all time,
In my soul she'll ever shine, tho' my heart be sore ;
Lies did me pursue—God knows my love for her 's true ;
Oh, I would die to save her from grief and woe!
Whatever be my station, in this great nation,
I'll ne'er forget that fair one—she's th' darling of my soul

WOMAN'S LOVE.

When a woman wants your love,
She will try to please you :
When a woman has your love,
She will try to tease you.
She will please you,
She will tease you.
When a woman wants your love
She will try to please you.

EPIGRAM.

Th' warrior fights for renown,
The poet writes for a name ;
A woman loves a silk gown,
And the miser gold and gain.

HARRIET DARLING.

I.

Don't you remember, Harriet darling,
When you stood by the apple-tree?
You looked so beautiful and charming,
There I fell in love with thee.
I will ne'er forget that morning,
For you are all the world to me ;
Oh, I love you, Harriet darling.
I'm always thinking, love, of thee.
Harriet, Harriet,
Don't you remember, Harriet darling,
When you stood by the apple-tree?

II.

Brighter than Phœbus in the morning,
With three rakes ye did stand ;
Ye looked so fair and enchanting,
So beautiful and grand.
I'll ne'er forget your gardening,
For ye were a lovely three ;
Oh, I love you, Harriet darling,
I'm always thinking, love, of thee.
Harriet, Harriet.
Don't you remember, Harriet darling, etc.

III.

Oh, love, don't you be alarming,
For I'm going you to see ;
Love, won't you greet me when calling,
And smile fondly upon me.
There is no goddess so charming,
You are dearer than life to me ;
Oh, I love you, Harriet darling,
I'm always thinking, love, of thee.
Harriet, Harriet.
Don't you remember, Harriet darling, etc.

HATTIE.

Air—"*Green Grow the Rushes, O!*"

I WILL ne'er forget the day,
    When I met little Hattie, O!
She look'd like an angel fair,
    Standing by her mamma, O!
        Dear little Hattie, O!
        Sweet little Hattie, O!
            The fairest maid in all the land
        Is lovely little Hattie, O!

Her eyes were like diamonds bright,
    Her hair hung down her shoulders, O!
Her hands were like the lily white,
    And her cheeks were like th' roses, O!
        Dear little Hattie, O! etc.

She's modest and she is meek,
    Beautiful and charming, O!
She's like an angel when she speaks,
    Is not she a darling, O!
        Dear little Hattie, O! etc.

GARFIELD HORSE.

GARFIELD horse has got a cough,
    And the do da, and the do da;
He has the spavin and the bots,
    And the do da, and the do da day.

I'm going to run all night,
  I'm going to run all day ;
I bet my money on the Hancock horse,
  Garfield horse will lose the day.

Garfield horse has lost his tail,
  And the do da, and the do da day ;
And his shoulder he did sprain,
  And the do da, and the do da day ;
    I'm going to run all night, etc.

The Garfield horse is not sound,
  And the do da, and the do da ;
He'll break his neck on the ground,
  And the do da, and the do da day.
    I'm going to run all night, etc.

Garfield horse is on a trot,
  And the do da, and the do da day ;
He'll soon be dead—let him rot,
  And the do da, and the do da day ;
    I'm going to run all night, etc.

GARFIELD JIMMY.

ALL you lads and lasses,
  Listen to my ditty ;
I will sing you a song,
  About Garfield Jimmy.
Tally hi ho, hi ho, tally hi ho the grinder.

In Washington city,
  Garfield made a blunder ;
He joined the Shepherd ring,
  And got some of the plunder.
    Tally hi ho, etc.

He took many strides,
  He was a nice jobber ;
The "dark horse" he rides,
  This salary grabber.
      Tally hi ho, etc.

Garfield is a great fraud,
  He is a deceiver ;
He soiled his big paw,
  With Credit Mobilier.
      Tally hi ho, etc.

The Buckeye statesman's
  "Brief" was a big dicker ;
With De Golyer man,
  He was a smart tricker.
      Tally hi ho, etc.

Jim won't be president,
  He is rather frail ;
On his country's flag,
  Did he not turn tail ?
      Tally hi ho, etc.

Old Garfield will be "beat,"
  The soldiers' vote will kill him ;
Their bill he did defeat,
  He is an old sinner.
      Tally hi ho, etc.

Garfield's heart is cold,
  He'll surely be beaten ;
The workingmen he sold,
  For the Chinese heathen.
      Tally hi ho, etc.

Let us have a change,
    Garfield wont be winner ;
The rings we will break,
    After next November.
        Tally hi ho, etc.

HANCOCK'S MARCH.

Hancocks are a fighting race,
    There is no race more bolder ;
For the " Red-coats " they did chase,
    From Tarrytown to Dover.
        Vote for Gen'l Hancock, boys,
            There is no man more bolder ;
        Vote for Gen'l Hancock, boys,
            The brave American soldier.

In the year seventy-six,
    The patriots did assemble ;
(——) Hancock his name did affix,
    Which made the British tremble ;
        Vote for Gen'l Hancock, boys, etc.

Hancock, in Mexico did fight,
    And on the field of slaughter,
Santa Anna he put to flight,
    And made the foe run faster.
        Vote for Gen'l Hancock, boys, etc.

In our recent civil strife,
    Midst slaughter and confusion ;
He fought to save th' nation's life,
    Liberty and the Union.
        Vote for Gen'l Hancock, boys, etc.

Gen'l Hancock will gain the day,
   On the seventh of November;
Corruption he will sweep away,
   And all the thieving ringers.
         Vote for Gen'l Hancock, boys, etc.

VOTE HANCOCK TRUE AND ENGLISH TOO.

Boys in blue be firm and true,
   Whatever be your station ;
Vote Hancock true and English too,
   Presidents of the nation.

Farmers you, be this your view,
   From "ringers" free the nation ;
Vote Hancock true and English too,
   Presidents of the nation.

Miners you, that day you'll rue,
   If Gar' gets into station ;
Vote Hancock true and English too,
   Presidents of the nation.

Tax payers you, heed this tune,
   "Sweep corruption from th' nation ;
Vote Hancock true and English too,
   Presidents of the nation.

Workmen you, this you will do,
   Without more hesitation ;
Vote Hancock true and English too,
   Presidents of the nation.

ANTI-RENTERS' MARCH.

Th' star of war now's advancing,
   And the brave sons of Mars,
Their steeds are all a prancing—
   And in freedom's noble cause,
We will all march together ;
   For to trample tyrants' laws,
We'll fight now and for ever.

Th' flowers of Erin now're blooming,
   And the brave sons of toil,
Their rights they are resuming—
   For our country and our right,
We'll march forward and steady ;
   For to vanquish tyrants' might,
We'll be loyal and ready.

God is th' Lord of all creation,
   And man is a man,
Whatever be his station !
   And Erin's brave bands
Now, now, are all a meeting ·
   For their homes and lands,
They will all fight defending.

Down with the laws o' extermination,
   And down with the rent,
All over the Irish nation ;
   Oh, you brave and you strong,
Of famine don't be expiring ;
   But to the battle throng,
And rather die a fighting.

Ireland's Hymn of Liberty.

Irish Air.

Sons of th' brave and free, rally from sea to sea,
    Your country for to make free, from shore to shore ;
Trample on th' despots power, tyrants we'll pull down,
    Heed not th' monarch's frown, now and for ever more ;
Fight, you sons of Erin, all o'er the nation,
    'Till Ireland takes her station, as in days of yore.

Behold your children's tears, and of your aged sires,
    Hearken to th' widows' cries, for famine is quite sore!
Rally from country and town, landlords we'll pull down,
    We'll trample on th' monarch's crown, we'll shed streams
        of gore ;
Rent and taxation, famine, and desolation,
    Shall ne'er oppress th' nation, while we've a pike or sword.

Off with the despot's yoke, down with the hireling hosts!
    We'll banish the foreign foe, as Brian did the Danes ;
Up with each stalwart man, vanquish the ruffian bands,
    We will possess th' land, as our fathers did before ;
No more transportation or extermination,
    Shall again scourge the nation, now or ever more.

Fear not the landlord's crew, fear not the titled few,
    Fear not the hirelings too, for man must be free.
Dungeons 'll have a fall, down with prison bars,
    Th' people will no more be thralls, we'll have liberty.
Rally with all your might, fight for human right,
    March! March! to the strife, to death or victory!

PRESIDENT GRANT.

Air—"*Wait for the Wagon.*"

ALL you loyal citizens,
　You will stand up in a row ;
And against the third termers,
　How merrily we will vote.
　　The old Galena tanner,
　　The old Galena tanner,
　　The old Galena tanner,
　　　Will come to grief and woe.

When Gen'l Grant was president,
　The jail-birds did loudly sing ;
He had around him drummers,
　Of the vile old whiskey ring.
　　The old Galena tanner, etc.

When Gen'l Grant was president,
　He trampled on right and law ;
He put Hayes into office,
　By bayonets, bribes, and fraud.
　　The old Galena tanner, etc.

Grant tramped his way in Europe,
　With the money of the ring ;
He wanted the people,
　To make him Sultan or King.
　　The old Galena tanner, etc.

The old Galena tanner.
　He shall never rule again ;
Grant and all the third termers,
　May now go to Pluto's den.
　　The old Galena tanner, etc.

THE CONFIDENCE MAN.

Eddy was the slyest fox,
　　From Vermont to Killarney ;
Mickey was the slyest dog,
　　That ever sipped the barley.

　　　To ra lo ral lam,
　　　To ra lo ral 'lam.

Old Mickey and a good man,
　　Were partners and were bankers ;
Mickey laid a deep plan,
　　The partner's gold he did hanker.
　　　To ra lo ral lam, etc.

But the good man passed away,
　　From this world and its bondage ;
He left his gold and bank they say,
　　With Ed. and Mick to manage.
　　　To ra lo ral lam, etc.

The widow and her children four,
　　Were in high expectations ;
Somebody's heart will yet be sore,
　　For Ed. and Mick's operations.
　　　To ra lo ral lam, etc.

A GIRL'S LOVE.

A girl loves her beau to meet,
　　She likes a song or a sonnet ;
She loves to promenade th' street,
　　With a new hat or a bonnet.